BUNNY BONANZA

Books in the Animal Ark Pets series

BEN M. BAGLIO

BUNNY BONANZA

Illustrations by
Paul Howard

Cover Illustration by
Chris Chapman

A
LITTLE APPLE
PAPERBACK

SCHOLASTIC INC.
New York Toronto London Auckland Sydney
Mexico City New Delhi Hong Kong

No part of this publication may be reproduced in whole or in part, or stored in a retrieval system, or transmitted in any form or by any means, electronic, mechanical, photocopying, recording, or otherwise, without written permission of the publisher. For information regarding permission, write to Scholastic Inc., 555 Broadway, New York, NY 10012.

ISBN 0-439-23024-1

Text copyright © 1998 by Working Partners Ltd.
Original series created by Ben M. Baglio.
Illustrations copyright © 1998 by Scholastic Inc.

All rights reserved. Published by Scholastic Inc.

SCHOLASTIC and associated logos are trademarks and/or registered trademarks of Scholastic Inc.

12 11 10 9 8 7 6 5 4 3 2   1 2 3 4 5 6/0

Printed in the U.S.A.   40
First Scholastic printing, March 2001

Contents

1

Exciting News

Mandy Hope shifted her schoolbag impatiently on her shoulder and waited for James Hunter to come out of Grade 3. He was in the class behind Mandy at school, but they were best friends and always walked home together. Today, James was late.

Mandy was eager to get back to Animal Ark to see if any new animals had come in. Animal Ark was the stone cottage where Mandy lived — and it was also her parents' veterinary clinic.

" 'Bye, Mandy," called two of her friends, Jill Redfern and Pam Stanton, as they walked past.

" 'Bye!" answered Mandy. "See you tomorrow."

A girl with round glasses and brown hair in braids wheeled her bike down the path. She was Jenny Carter, a new girl in James's class. Jenny's mother bred Netherland Dwarf rabbits and one of them was due to have babies any day. "Hello, Jenny," Mandy called out, hurrying after her. "Has Clover had her babies yet?"

Jenny shook her head. "No, not yet. Mom thought she might have them today."

"Fingers crossed." Mandy laughed.

Jenny nodded, her eyes shining. "I can't wait! Mom said that I can choose one to keep."

"Lucky you!" sighed Mandy. Her mom and dad were so busy looking after other people's animals that Mandy couldn't have a pet of her own. But she did get to meet all the animals that came into the busy vets' practice.

"I don't know how I'm going to decide," said Jenny. "I know I'll want them all! Anyway, see you tomorrow, Mandy."

Jenny hurried off just as James came running out of the school doors. His brown hair flopped over his eyes and his glasses slipped down his nose. "Sorry I was so long," he explained, pushing his glasses back on to his nose, "but Mrs. Black was showing me this new book about computers." James loved computers nearly as much as he loved animals, and he loved animals nearly as much as Mandy did.

"That's okay," said Mandy. "Let's go. I want to see what's happened today at Animal Ark!"

At the village square, Mandy and James went their separate ways — James toward his house at the end of the village, and Mandy to Animal Ark.

She ran up the path and in through the clinic

door. Emily Hope, Mandy's mother, was talking on the telephone.

"I'm sure everything is okay, Mrs. Carter," she was saying. Mandy tiptoed up to the desk. "Keep a careful eye on her. If you notice anything out of the ordinary then call us. But I'm sure everything will be just fine. The babies will be here soon." She said good-bye and put down the phone. "That was Jenny's mom," she explained to Mandy.

Mandy looked anxious. "Why was she calling? Clover is okay, isn't she?"

Dr. Emily nodded. "It's the first time one of Mrs. Carter's rabbits has been late giving birth, and she just wanted me to tell her that everything was all right."

"Oh," said Mandy. "I wish Clover's babies would hurry up."

Dr. Emily pushed a strand of red hair back into her ponytail. "They'll be here soon enough, Mandy. Nature won't be rushed!"

Mandy dumped her bag on the floor. "Have any animals come in today?" she asked.

"One of Mrs. Lawson's Labradors came in to have his hips x-rayed," her mom said.

"But he is all right, isn't he?" Mandy asked.

"Oh, yes." Dr. Emily nodded. "Do you want to come and see him?"

"Of course!" said Mandy.

Mandy wasn't allowed to help with the sick animals that stayed at the clinic until she was twelve — three whole years away. However, she was allowed to talk to and fuss over the animals that weren't too ill.

She followed her mom into the residential unit. A large black Labrador lay on a white fluffy rug in one of the cages. He wagged his tail when he heard them come in.

"He's a bit sleepy still," Dr. Emily explained. "He had to have an anesthetic so we could get his legs into exactly the right place for the X ray."

Mandy crouched down to tickle the Labrador's ears through the wire. "What was the matter with his hips?" she asked.

"Nothing," Dr. Emily told her. "But Mrs.

Lawson is thinking of breeding him and if you are going to breed big dogs you need to check that their hip bones are healthy. Otherwise, there's a chance that the faulty hips will be inherited by the puppies. Responsible owners always take their dogs for a thorough checkup before they start breeding."

"I'm glad he's all right," said Mandy. "He really looks like Blackie, don't you think?" Blackie was James's young Labrador. He was only a puppy and still very naughty.

"They're probably related," said Dr. Emily. "After all, Mrs. Lawson bred Blackie just like she bred this fellow here."

"I bet James would like to see him," said Mandy. "Will he still be here tomorrow?"

Dr. Emily shook her head. "He's going home in half an hour."

Mandy opened the cage door and knelt down beside the Labrador. "I'll tell James all about you," she said to the dog as she gently stroked his head.

Dr. Emily let Mandy talk to him and then said that they should leave him to sleep off the effects of the anesthetic before Mrs. Lawson arrived to get him.

"So what are you going to do now?" Dr. Emily asked as they went back to the waiting room.

"Do you think I could go and see Clover?" Mandy asked hopefully.

Dr. Emily looked thoughtful. "Well, I was going to ask you to take a book around to Grandma's. I got it today in Walton for her, but

I suppose you could stop in to see Clover on the way." Her voice took on a note of warning. "But only if Mrs. Carter doesn't mind, and *only* if you promise just to have a *quick* look. Animals need to be left in peace before they give birth. You mustn't disturb Clover."

"Of course I won't," said Mandy. She knew that you always had to think of animals first. "I promise."

Mandy followed Mrs. Carter and Jenny down the yard to the large, airy shed where the rabbits' hutches were kept. They passed the other four rabbits hopping around in their runs. "That's Lettuce and that's Carrots," said Jenny, pointing out the rabbits to Mandy. "And Smoky and Honey are in this run over here. They're all pedigree Dwarfs, but Clover's the most valuable of the lot. Isn't she, Mom?"

Mrs. Carter nodded. "Yes, and she's won quite a few prizes."

Mandy didn't care how much an animal was

worth or how many prizes it had won — to her they were all special.

They entered the shed. Clover was sitting in her hutch nibbling at a pile of sweet-smelling hay. Like the other Dwarf rabbits, she had short little ears and large round eyes. Her glossy black coat was flecked with silver around her tummy, her paws, and inside her ears. Her nose never seemed to stop twitching.

"She's so sweet," Mandy said, gazing longingly through the wire mesh of the hutch. "I hope she has her babies soon."

"If it's sunny tomorrow, I'll put her out in

the yard for a while," Mrs. Carter said. "There's an old run in the garage. Maybe sitting in the sun will hurry her along."

"Yes, she'll like that," said Mandy, pleased.

Remembering the promise to her mom, Mandy made sure that she only stayed for a few minutes. Then she set off to her grandma and grandpa's. When she arrived at Lilac Cottage, Grandpa was in the garden carefully trimming dead flowers off a camellia bush.

"I've got a book for Grandma," Mandy said, leaning her bike against the wall and getting it out of her backpack. It was called *Walks in the Lake District*. "Are you going to the Lake District?" she asked.

"Your grandma wants to," Grandpa said, but he didn't sound very enthusiastic. Grandma loved traveling but Mandy sometimes thought that secretly Grandpa would rather stay at home in his garden. "I suppose I'd better take it in to her," he said.

"I'll take it," Mandy offered.

Grandma was in the kitchen, surrounded by a mountain of dirty dishes. A delicious smell of baking hung in the air.

Mandy sniffed. "Mmm, ginger cookies!"

"And muffins, apple tart, and chocolate cake," said Grandma, nodding toward the wire trays piled high on the side. "How are you?"

"Fine," said Mandy, giving her a hug. "What are you baking for?"

"I don't need a reason for baking," Grandma said, with a laugh. "It's always handy to have some supplies in the freezer just in case."

"In case of *what*?" Mandy asked.

"You never know when cookies and cakes will be needed," said Grandma wisely.

Mandy picked up a dish towel and started to help Grandma dry. She told Grandma all about Clover. "I just hope she has her babies soon. She's so lovely."

Grandma's eyes twinkled. "But you think *all* animals are lovely, Mandy!"

Mandy grinned. She hastily rescued a mixing bowl just as Grandma was about to dip it in the soapy water. "That's not ready to be washed yet, Grandma," she said, running her finger around the inside and licking it.

Grandma laughed. "Cleaning up the Mandy way!" She dried her hands. "Come on, I'll finish up later. I've got my badminton lesson in half an hour and I've got to get ready. Why don't you go and get yourself a glass of lemonade while I get changed?"

Mandy washed the bowl and her sticky fingers and poured herself a glass of ice-cold lemonade from the fridge. She sat down at the sturdy kitchen table. Grandpa had left his copy of the *Walton Gazette* on the table. Mandy folded it up neatly. As she was doing so, something in the newspaper caught her eye.

ARE YOU AN ANIMAL LOVER?

Mandy opened the paper. As she read the advertisement, her eyes widened and her heart began to thump with excitement.

ARE YOU AN ANIMAL LOVER?

Will you stand up and be counted?

On Easter Saturday, animal lovers all over the country will be holding a variety of fund-raising events to support Animal Welfare.

If you would like to be one of them, and if you have a fun, original idea for an event, then why not fill in the form below and apply to be registered as an official fund-raiser?

Certificates will be provided for all registered events. Prove that you really are an animal lover — join "We Love Animals Day"!

(Mail entries only.)

Grandma came back into the kitchen in her track suit. "Okay, I'm all ready. . . . Why, whatever's the matter, Mandy?" she said in surprise as Mandy jumped up, waving the newspaper at her.

"Animal lovers have to stand up and be counted!" Mandy shrieked. "Look, it says so here, Grandma. There's going to be a 'We Love Animals Day.' James and I have to think of an idea! Can I have this page of the paper, please?"

"Yes, of course. Mandy, calm down —"

But Mandy was already halfway out of the door. She had to tell James the exciting news. "'Bye, Grandpa!" she shouted as she tore down the path.

"What's the rush?" Grandpa called after her.

"I'm going to stand up and be counted!" gasped Mandy. Jumping on her bike, she set off as fast as she could down the road.

2

Mandy to the Rescue

Mandy and James read and reread the now rather crumpled piece of newspaper. Blackie tried to get their attention by jumping up and nibbling the edges of the page.

"Get off, Blackie," said Mandy, holding it out of his reach. "Isn't it great?" she said. "Just think of all the money we could raise for animals." Her eyes shone. Blackie sensed Mandy's excitement and jumped up again.

"Blackie, *down!*" James ordered, pushing Blackie away.

"Obedient as ever!" said Mandy with a grin.

"*Worse* than ever," corrected James. "He keeps chewing things he shouldn't."

Mandy looked at the piece of newspaper. "What are we going to do, James? It's got to be something really original, so lots of people want to come. The more people, the more money!"

"It has to be something so good that people can have certificates for it," James said. He was pointing to the line in the ad that said the organization would provide certificates.

"But *what?*" asked Mandy.

"Maybe your mom and dad will have some ideas," suggested James. "Let's go to Animal Ark."

For once there had been no emergency calls, and both Dr. Adam and Dr. Emily were in the clinic's reception. They were discussing the day's cases. Jean Knox, the clinic's receptionist, was filing paperwork, her glasses perched on the end of her nose. Simon, the clinic nurse, was mopping the floor with disinfectant, a job that had to be done regularly. They all looked up as Mandy and James burst through the door.

"We're going to organize an event!" announced Mandy, her eyes shining. "For Animal Welfare. We've got to think of a really good idea. We're going to raise lots of money."

"Slow down!" said Dr. Emily, holding up her hands and laughing. "Now, what's all this?"

Mandy and James explained more slowly. "It's got to be a fun, original idea," Mandy said. "Look, it says so here."

Dr. Adam took the advertisement from Mandy and read through it. Dr. Emily and Jean peered over his shoulder. "Well, it looks like it's for a worthwhile cause," he said.

"But we can't think of anything to do," said James.

"How about a sponsored dog walk?" suggested Jean.

"Not original or exciting enough," said Simon, leaning on his mop. "What about a duck race?"

"Yes!" Mandy cried. "We could ask Mr. Marsh from Woodbridge Farm Park if we could use his ducks."

"Hang on!" interrupted Dr. Adam. "A duck race isn't with real ducks — it's with wooden ducks or rubber ducks down a stream. There'd be chaos if you had live ducks."

"Oh," said Mandy, looking disappointed. A duck race had sounded fun, but not one with ducks that weren't real. "It has to be something with *real* animals," she said.

"Well, what about a sponsored weight loss for pets?" suggested Dr. Adam. "Far too many people let their pets get overweight."

"That's a bit difficult to do in one day," Simon pointed out.

Dr. Emily smiled and patted her husband's rather round stomach. "Pity, we could have included a sponsored weight loss for husbands."

Mandy grinned at her dad. He didn't seem to think that was a good idea at all!

"It should really have something to do with Easter," said Dr. Emily thoughtfully. "After all, it is going to be on Easter Saturday."

Mandy nodded.

James was looking at the ad. "It says here that ideas have to be in by next Tuesday."

Mandy quickly counted on her fingers. "That's only four days away."

Dr. Adam put his arm around her shoulders. "You'll think of something," he said.

"I hope so!" said Mandy, looking up at him.

Saturday's clinic was always busy. Mandy loved talking to all the animals — calming the frightened ones, and fussing over the friendly ones.

Today, Sooty, Blackie's litter brother, was in to have a kennel cough vaccination. He jumped up at Mandy, his pink tongue desperately trying to lick her face.

"How's his training going?" Mandy asked Sarah Drummond, his owner. Sarah was in the same class as Mandy.

"It's not!" Sarah laughed. "Can't you tell?"

There was little Laura Baker with her rabbit, Patch, who had come in because he needed his teeth trimmed. Reverend Hadcroft was also there, with his tabby cat Jemima, in for her annual booster shot.

Mandy fussed over all the animals and talked

to their owners. Seeing Patch made her think about Clover. Had she had her babies yet? Mandy couldn't wait. She decided to go over and find out. After all, there were a few baby carrots in the fridge that she was sure her Mom wouldn't miss. They would be a perfect present for Clover!

Jenny saw Mandy coming eagerly up the path and she came outside to meet her. "I've brought some carrots for Clover," said Mandy. "Has she had her babies?"

"Not yet," answered Jenny.

"Oh," said Mandy, disappointed.

Mrs. Carter came to the door. "Hi, Mandy," she said, smiling. "Clover's out in the old run at the bottom of the yard. "It's a bit shabby, but I'm not going to leave her out there for long. You can take your carrots to her if you like."

Mandy and Jenny stopped to say hello to the other rabbits. They snuffled hopefully at the carrots through the wire mesh of their runs. "I'd better give them something as well or

they'll get jealous," Jenny said. "There's some cabbage in the shed. Clover's down there if you want to go and see her."

Mandy set off down the path. Suddenly a high, squealing cry ripped through the quiet air. Mandy froze. The sound made the hairs prickle on the back of her neck. It was a cry of pain and terror, and it was coming from the bottom of the yard.

"Clover!" Mandy gasped. Dropping the carrots, she raced down the path.

A terrifying sight met her eyes. One section of the wire mesh of Clover's run had come loose and a large black-and-white cat was squeezing through the gap. The little rabbit was cowering at the back of the run, her ears back, her eyes terrified, as the cat inched closer and closer. Clover threw her head back and squealed again.

"NO!" shouted Mandy. She tore over to the cage. "Go away! Get back."

The cat shot backward out of the gap and streaked across the grass and over the garden wall. Clover's body jerked, and she collapsed on her side, trembling all over, her eyes shut.

"Jenny! Mrs. Carter!" shouted Mandy. "Come quick!"

The gravel flew up from under Mandy's bicycle tires. Mrs. Carter and Jenny were following in the car with Clover. Mandy had gone on ahead to tell her dad about the emergency. Her breath came in short gasps as she pedaled frantically. Clover had to be okay, she *had* to be!

As soon as Dr. Adam heard about Clover, he

finished with the patient he was seeing. "Get hold of Emily," he told Jean. Dr. Emily would need to take over the clinic while Dr. Adam tried to help Clover.

Mandy was anxiously watching the driveway. "They're here!" she called.

Mrs. Carter and Jenny hurried across the gravel, Mrs. Carter carrying a cardboard box. Mandy opened the door wide for her.

Dr. Adam looked into the box. "She's having her babies," he said grimly. "Quick, bring her through."

Mrs. Carter hurried through into the operating room. The door shut firmly behind her.

3

Bunny Babies

Mandy and Jenny waited in the office. Mandy's heart was pounding and she felt sick, but she knew she had to be brave. She wanted to be a vet when she grew up, and her dad always said that vets had to keep calm in emergencies. She squeezed Jenny's hand. "Clover will be okay," she told her. "You'll see." Jenny nodded, but tears ran down her cheeks.

Mrs. Carter came to join them. Her face was pale. Mandy didn't know what to say. She went to the kitchen and made three cups of tea and carried them back on a tray. "Here you are," she offered.

Mrs. Carter managed a faint smile. "Thank you, Mandy," she said gratefully.

Mandy looked at her worried face. "Don't worry, Mrs. Carter," she said. "Clover will be all right. I know she will. Dad will help her."

Mrs. Carter nodded, but her face looked strained.

Mandy sat down. She watched the minute hand tick around on the clock — it seemed to be moving so slowly. All she could think about was poor little Clover. What if she didn't survive?

At last the door opened, and Dr. Adam walked in. Mandy jumped up anxiously. What was the news?

"Everything's okay," Dr. Adam announced,

his face breaking into a smile. "Clover's going to be fine."

Mrs. Carter gave a cry of joy and Jenny burst into tears again. Mandy ran over and threw her arms around her dad's waist. "Oh, Dad!" she cried happily.

"It was touch-and-go for a while," said Dr. Adam, "but I think she's over the worst now."

"And what about the babies?" asked Mrs. Carter.

"Ten," said Dr. Adam. "All fine."

"Ten!" exclaimed the girls.

Dr. Adam's eyes twinkled. "Yes, ten," he said.

"Can we see them?" asked Jenny.

"Just quickly," said Dr. Adam. "Clover is still quite weak and she won't be able to go home for a few days yet. But I think I can let you and your mom have one little peep."

"And Mandy," said Mrs. Carter quickly. "She's been a tower of strength."

Dr. Adam nodded and showed them through. As Mandy walked past him, he stopped her for a second. "Well done," he said softly.

Mandy glowed with pride as she followed Jenny and her mom.

They tiptoed into the operating room. Clover lay sleeping in a warm box, her ten little babies curled up next to her.

"Oh, look at them all," breathed Mrs. Carter.

The babies were gray and each was about the size of a matchbox. They lay snuggled together. They didn't have any fur yet — that would grow in later.

Mandy stared at the babies. They looked so tiny and helpless but, thankfully, they were safe.

"I'm so glad Clover and her babies are all right," said Mandy as she ate supper with her mom and dad. "Can you pass the bread please, Dad? Poor little Clover, she must have had such a scare." She didn't think she would ever forget the sight of the cat squeezing through the wire and Clover screaming. "It was horrible."

"The cat was only behaving naturally," said Dr. Adam, passing her the bread. "Animals instinctively hunt each other. And sometimes it's

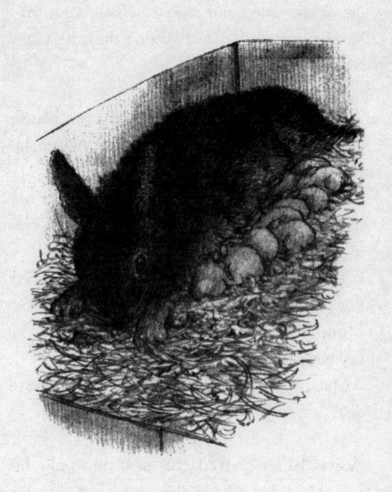

necessary — if foxes didn't kill wild rabbits, there would be too many of them with not enough food to go around. They would start to die of starvation and disease, which is a horrible, long, slow death. It wasn't the cat's fault, Mandy. It's just nature's way."

Mandy sighed. "I know."

Dr. Emily started to clear away the plates. "Have you and James had any ideas yet for the Animal Welfare event?" she asked.

"No," said Mandy. "But he's coming over tomorrow. Maybe we'll think of one then. The idea doesn't have to be in till Tuesday."

"If the idea has to be in by Tuesday," pointed out Dr. Emily, "you'll have to mail the form on Monday morning. It said mail entries only in the newspaper, remember."

Mandy looked at her in horror. "By Monday! Oh, help!"

When James arrived the next morning he found Mandy in the kitchen, with bits of paper spread all around her. She'd written down lots of ideas, but crossed them all out. "We're just going to have to do a sponsored dog walk like Jean suggested," Mandy said in exasperation. "I can't think of anything else!"

James looked doubtful. "But what if they don't think it's a good enough idea?"

"They will," said Mandy, but she didn't sound very convinced.

"Your mom said it should be something to do with Easter," James reminded her.

"Well we can't exactly have a sponsored chicken walk, can we?" said Mandy. They both started to giggle at the idea.

"Hello, James," said Dr. Emily, coming into the kitchen. "I guess Mandy's told you all about Clover's babies?"

James nodded. "Can I see them?"

"Yes, Simon's in with them at the moment," said Dr. Emily. "You can go in now, if you like."

"They're doing well," Simon said as Mandy and James tiptoed through the door. They peered in the box where the baby rabbits lay all snuggled up together. "They should be ready to go home in a few days."

"Look at them all!" James said. He stared at the babies, his eyes getting wider and wider. "I've never seen so many baby rabbits before, ever!" he added in astonishment. "It's a . . . it's a bunny bonanza!"

Simon laughed. "An Easter bunny bonanza," he agreed. "They'll be going to their new homes by then, so they'll be proper little Easter bunnies!"

Mandy stared at them. A bunny bonanza? Her heart began to race. She'd just thought of something. Lots of rabbits, all at Easter . . .

"I think I've got an idea for our event!" she gasped. "A really *brilliant* idea!"

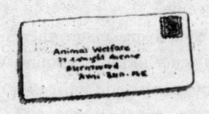

4

The Brilliant Idea

"So, you see," Mandy explained to James, Simon, and Dr. Adam, "it's simple — everyone with a rabbit can pay to bring their rabbit to a Bunny Bonanza. We can hold it at the village square and take a photograph of all the rabbits together. Everyone who comes can have a certificate. What do you think?" She looked around eagerly.

"I like it," said Simon, nodding in approval.

"It's really good," said James. "I bet we get loads of people."

"We'll have to make sure there's plenty of shade and water in case it's sunny. We should take lots of carrots and cabbage for the rabbits and we can put out runs . . ." continued Mandy, getting carried away in her excitement.

Dr. Adam looked a bit concerned. "You'll have to be careful that the rabbits don't get upset, Mandy. Rabbits do panic quite easily."

Mandy nodded. "We'll be *very* careful. And you and Mom and Simon could help. You could be there just in case anything went wrong, couldn't you?"

Dr. Adam nodded. "As long as it's after morning office hours, I imagine we could. I don't suppose there will be *that* many rabbits there. It will take a bit of organizing, though."

"But we're good at organizing, aren't we, James?" said Mandy.

James nodded. "We've organized for Paul and Paddy to get a special rosette at the Pony Club show, and for Harvey the gerbil to become our class pet, and for Joey to be able to keep Scruff and . . ."

"Yes, I guess you *are* good at organizing!" Dr. Adam laughed. "But don't get too excited, until you know your idea has been accepted."

"It will be!" said Mandy, her eyes glowing. "I just know it!"

Mandy and James sat down at the kitchen table. Mandy carefully filled in the details on the form. Names of organizers — that was easy. Name of event — Bunny Bonanza. Description of event — a gathering of rabbits from the village for one big photograph.

Dr. Adam had to sign the bottom; then Mandy and James walked to the mailbox. Mandy kissed the envelope. "Please be accepted," she whispered.

The wait for the reply was horrible. Every morning, when Mandy heard Bill Ward, the mailman, arrive, she dashed downstairs, but every morning it was the same. No reply on the mat. Just boring-looking letters for Dr. Adam and Dr. Emily.

As the days passed, Mandy started to feel less confident. What if Animal Welfare didn't accept her idea? What if it wasn't good enough?

She tried to keep her mind off the subject by

visiting Clover and her babies whenever she was allowed. Clover was a very good mother: she cleaned and fed and looked after her babies, and never left any of them out. After almost two weeks, their eyes had started to open and their fur was beginning to grow. Mandy couldn't imagine anything more adorable than the ten little furry bundles with their twitching noses and tiny ears.

"They're looking well, aren't they?" said Mrs. Carter proudly as she stood behind Mandy, James, and Jenny. They were all watching the babies feeding from Clover.

"I wish we could hold them," said Jenny longingly.

"You know you mustn't until they leave the nest," explained Mrs. Carter.

"Why not?" asked James.

Mandy knew. "It's because Clover might kill them if we did, isn't it, Mrs. Carter?" she said.

"That's right, Mandy. Mother rabbits don't like anyone handling their babies when they are still little. But it will be all right when they start moving around on their own. Then she won't mind."

"When will that be?" asked James.

"Normally when they are about sixteen days old," said Mrs. Carter. "So there are only a few more days to wait now."

"Three more," said Mandy. "They're thirteen days old today."

"Have you got homes for them yet?" James asked Mrs. Carter.

"Yes, for just about all of them," said Mrs. Carter. "They'll be going to their new homes just after Easter."

"Will you bring them to our Bunny Bonanza before they go?" Mandy asked eagerly. She suddenly remembered and looked worried. "If our idea is accepted, of course," she added.

The letter arrived the very next day. Mandy raced down the stairs as usual and there, lying on the mat, was a thick cream-colored envelope. It was addressed to "Miss M. Hope."

On the front were the words "Animal Welfare."

"Any interesting mail?" Dr. Emily asked, coming through from the kitchen. She saw the envelope in Mandy's hand. "So it's finally arrived. Aren't you going to open it?"

Mandy just stared at the letter. What if it said no?

"Go on, Mandy," Dr. Emily encouraged her. "Open it up."

Mandy looked at the envelope for a moment longer. Then, taking a deep breath, she ripped open the top and pulled the letter out. Her fingers trembled as she unfolded it. Her eyes skimmed the top line of the letter.

Dear Mandy,
We are delighted to tell you . . .

Mandy gasped with excitement. "They've said yes!" she squealed, waving the letter and jumping up and down. "Oh, Mom, Mom. They've said yes!"

Dr. Emily hugged her. Mandy couldn't stop jumping up and down. "I've *got* to tell James!" she cried. "Just wait till he hears. We've got *so* much to do! It's going to be the best Bunny Bonanza ever!"

5

Blackie in Trouble

"We need to make a plan," said James. "We should write up a list."

James had come around as soon as he could after Mandy had called to tell him the exciting news. They sat at the kitchen table in Animal Ark drinking juice and eating chips. Mandy got out some paper and a pen. "We've got to make posters," she said. "And get forms for people to fill in."

"We'll need containers to put people's entry money in," James added.

"And for the rabbits' food and water," said Mandy. "It would be good to have runs as well, so the rabbits don't have to stay in their carriers."

James frowned. "But where would we get them from?"

"We could ask everyone we know with a rabbit or a guinea pig," said Mandy. "I'm sure they wouldn't mind lending their runs for one day."

"We'll need labels, to show that people have paid," said James. "Dad's got loads of white stickers at home. We could decorate a corner of each sticker with a rabbit."

"Good idea!" said Mandy, feeling pleased. She started to write a list:

Things to Do for the Bunny Bonanza
  1. Rabbit food
  2. Rabbit runs

3. Containers for water/money
4. Entry forms and labels
5. Posters

Dr. Emily came into the kitchen. She was pinning her hair up, ready to go out on her afternoon rounds. "What are you two up to?" she asked.

"We're deciding what we need to do for the Bunny Bonanza," Mandy told her happily.

"And there's plenty!" added James.

"You'll just have to delegate," said Dr. Emily.

James frowned. "Delegate? Does that mean spread things out?"

"That's right. You've got lots of friends; I'm sure they'll all help." Dr. Emily looked over Mandy's shoulder at the list. "If you are going to have runs for the rabbits," she warned, "you'd better have some rules. People must only put rabbits together if the rabbits are healthy and have been vaccinated. And they mustn't put two males together who don't know each other because they might fight.

You'll also need to make sure that people don't put unneutered males and females together."

"Because they might mate and have babies," said Mandy.

Dr. Emily nodded. "Maybe you should make a sign warning people about those things."

Mandy added it to her list.

"I could do it," said James. "There's some spare wood in our garage, and I could type out a notice on my computer."

"You'll also have to ask the City Council's permission to use the village square," Dr. Emily told them.

"But I thought we could just use it," said Mandy.

Dr. Emily shook her head. "For something like this you'll have to ask Mr. Markham. He's the chairman of the City Council. He lives just off High Street." Her green eyes looked thoughtful. "I've got a house call near there this afternoon. I could see if he's in and ask him for you, if you like."

"Oh, could you, Mom?" said Mandy, relieved. But she added it to the list, just the same.

"There you are," said Dr. Emily with a smile, going out of the room. "*That's* delegation!"

Mandy turned to James. "I hope Mr. Markham says yes."

James looked worried. "What are we going to do if he doesn't?"

"Find somewhere else, I suppose," said Mandy. She bit her lip. She had a feeling it would be difficult to find somewhere else to hold the Bunny Bonanza.

To take their minds off waiting to hear what Mr. Markham said, Mandy and James decided to go to James's house to pick up the stickers. "We can get Blackie while we're there," said James. "He needs a walk."

On the way there they met Jenny Carter. "Where are you going?" Mandy asked her.

"To Amy's," said Jenny. Amy Fenton was in Grade 3 with Jenny and James. She had a white mouse called Minnie. "I'm having a snack there. Then Amy's coming back to my house to see the babies. She's trying to persuade her mom to let her have one. What about you?"

Mandy and James explained about going to get the stickers for the Bunny Bonanza. "We've got loads to do," said James.

Mandy suddenly remembered what her mom had said about sharing the jobs. "Would you like to help us, Jenny?" she asked.

Jenny looked delighted. "I'd love to. What do you want me to do?"

Mandy thought for a moment. "You could help us make the posters," she suggested. "We want to get them up as soon as possible. That way, lots of people will see them and come to the event."

"Amy and I could do them this afternoon," said Jenny eagerly. "She's got a really good computer. It does great pictures, and it prints in color. What do you want on them?"

Mandy tore a piece of paper from her notepad and wrote down the details. "Thanks, Jenny!"

"We'll bring them into school on Monday," said Jenny, hurrying off. " 'Bye!"

James and Mandy started walking. "Delegation," Mandy said with a grin.

When they got to James's house, Mrs. Hunter greeted them at the door with a half-eaten wastepaper basket in one hand. "Honestly, James, I don't know what we are going to do with that dog," she said crossly. "Look what he's done now!"

Blackie ran to say hello to James and Mandy. Then he jumped up excitedly at the wastepaper basket. He seemed to think it was a great toy.

James quickly grabbed Blackie's collar. "Sorry, Mom."

"It's got to stop," said Mrs. Hunter seriously. "He's already chewed a shoe, two pens, and a library book this week."

"We'll think of something," promised James.

Mandy held firmly on to Blackie while James ran to his bedroom. When he returned, they hurried Blackie out of the house.

"Your mom wasn't too happy," said Mandy. She looked at Blackie, who was trotting happily along on his leash. "You've been a naughty boy, Blackie," she said, tapping his nose. Blackie just wagged his tail.

"He's chewing everything at the moment," said James gloomily. "I don't know what to do. Mom's getting really annoyed."

"We could ask my mom," said Mandy. "She's bound to think of something."

When they got back to Animal Ark, they found that Dr. Emily had gone out on her afternoon rounds. "We'll ask her when she gets back," said Mandy.

They set out the labels on the kitchen table. Blackie put his paws on the table to see what they were doing. "Blackie, get down!" said James, pushing him off.

Blackie went around the table to see what Mandy was doing. He put his head on her lap

and wagged his tail hard. She giggled. "Blackie, go away, we're busy!"

Then Blackie picked up a felt-tip pen and ran off with it. James got it back from him before he could eat it. "We'll never get these done with him here!" he said. "Oh, Blackie, what are we going to do with you?"

Blackie jumped up at him, knocking Mandy's arm.

"I think we'd better do the stickers in the living room," suggested Mandy. "We can leave Blackie in here and take him for a walk when we've finished."

It was much easier getting the labels done without Blackie's help. They quickly drew little rabbits in the corner of each one. "That's fifty labels," said Mandy, counting them at last. "That should be plenty."

A car pulled up outside. "That sounds like Mom," said Mandy, putting the lid on her felt-tip pen.

They heard the back door opening. Then they heard a cry.

Mandy and James looked at each other in alarm.

The living room door opened. Dr. Emily stood there, hands on her hips. "Would someone like to explain to me exactly *what* Blackie has been doing?"

6

Will They Come?

Mandy and James followed Dr. Emily through to the kitchen.

"Oh!" exclaimed Mandy, her hand flying to her mouth.

"Oh, no," said James.

The kitchen floor was covered with shredded paper towels, two chewed wooden spoons, and a trail of salt. Blackie stood in the middle of the mess, wagging his tail.

Dr. Emily picked up a rather mangled salt container with no top. "He must have jumped up and pulled the salt, paper towels, and spoons off the shelf," she said.

"Oh, dear," said James again, starting to pick up pieces of paper towel.

"We're really sorry, Mom," said Mandy, quickly helping him. "We didn't hear a thing. We'll clean it all up."

"Well, I guess there's no real harm done," sighed Dr. Emily, getting an empty trash bag. "At least he didn't chew anything that could have hurt him."

"He's been chewing *everything* at home," James told her as they cleaned up. "Mom's getting really angry."

"Labradors often do chew a lot," explained Dr. Emily. "Particularly when they're Blackie's age. You need to get him something of his own to chew on."

"He's got loads of toys," said James, "but he doesn't seem to want to chew those."

"Just your mom's shoes," said Mandy.

James nodded unhappily.

"In that case, you'll have to get him a toy that will really interest him," Dr. Emily said. "You can get dog toys with a hollow center. If you stuff the hole with treats — say, little dog biscuits — then the dog will chew the toy to get the food out."

"Hey, that's a great idea!" said Mandy.

"I bet Blackie would be interested in a toy like that," said James. "He's so greedy. I'm sure it would stop him from chewing Mom's things."

"Particularly if she buys some Bitter Spray," said Dr. Emily. "It tastes horrible to dogs. She can spray it on anything she doesn't want him to chew, and then you can give him his stuffed toy to keep him busy. But if you are going to give him a toy like that, remember to cut down his meals a bit so he doesn't get too fat. Blackie's in good condition at the moment — make sure he stays that way."

"Oh, I will," promised James.

"Mrs. McFarlane at the general store might have some dog toys with a hole in them," Mandy suggested. "She has everything."

"We could go and see," said James. "But only when we've finished cleaning up, of course," he added quickly.

Dr. Emily smiled at them. "Go on, you can go now. It's nearly done. It just needs a little vacuuming, and somehow I think that job is probably going to be easier with Blackie *out* of the way."

"Thanks, Dr. Emily!" said James, jumping to his feet.

"Before you go," said Dr. Emily as they reached the door, "I asked Mr. Markham about using the village square for the Bunny Bonanza."

"Oh, what did he say?" Mandy asked, spinning around suddenly.

"Well . . ." Dr. Emily teased.

"*Mom!*"

Dr. Emily smiled. "Relax. He said yes."

James and Mandy ran all the way to the general store. It was their favorite shop in the village. The shelves were always overflowing with interesting things — comics, candy, games, toys, and pet things.

"There's bound to be a toy with a hole in it in here," said Mandy as they tied up Blackie outside.

Mrs. McFarlane was standing behind the counter in her blue overalls. "What can I get you today?" she asked as they burst through the door. "Some lemon sherbet?"

"We need something special for Blackie," said Mandy.

James explained.

"I think I've got just the thing," Mrs. McFarlane said, getting the stepladder out. "Now, let me see." She rummaged around and pulled out a box from the top shelf. "How about one of these?"

In the box were five different-sized, thick

rubber toys. They were all oval-shaped with a hollow middle.

"They look perfect!" said Mandy.

"But which size should I get?" said James.

"One of the biggest ones," said Mandy. "You don't want Blackie to be able to choke on it."

James picked out a red one. "This one, then," he said. As he took out his money, Mandy told Mrs. McFarlane all about the Bunny Bonanza.

"It's going to be at the village square," she explained. "On Easter Saturday. It's for Animal Welfare, and James and I are organizing it. We're going to have runs for the rabbits to play in and then a big photograph at three o'clock."

Mrs. McFarlane was very interested. "It sounds like a wonderful idea. Would you like some old vegetables for the rabbits? My friend runs a grocery in Walton. She always has some left over on the weekends."

"Yes, please," said Mandy. "That would be great, Mrs. McFarlane! And can we put a poster up here when they're done? We want to get as many people as possible to come."

"Of course," said Mrs. McFarlane. "Have you thought about asking Reverend Hadcroft if you can put one up on the church bulletin board?"

"No, but it's a good idea," said Mandy. "Thanks, Mrs. McFarlane!"

James paid for the toy and they left the general store. "That's good," said Mandy, pleased.

"That's food for the rabbits *and* two places to put up posters."

"There's the school bulletin board as well, of course," added James. "And Animal Ark."

"I wonder what the posters will be like," said Mandy. "I can't wait to find out!"

Jenny and Amy were waiting excitedly for them at the school gates on Monday morning. "Look, we've done the posters," said Jenny, pulling a bundle of paper out of her schoolbag. Each of the posters had a picture of ten rabbits in a wheelbarrow. Big letters at the top said BUNNY BONANZA and then under the picture Jenny and Amy had typed the details of the day and time, and who to contact. The edge of the poster was decorated with little rabbits as well.

"Do you like them?" Amy asked, with a big smile.

"They're terrific," said Mandy.

"Really good!" agreed James. "Let's go and put one up on the bulletin board right away!"

By lunchtime, everyone in the school was talking about the Bunny Bonanza. Mandy and James had to answer lots of questions, such as what people would have to do and what the certificates looked like.

"You just have to bring a rabbit," Mandy said. "And we don't know what the certificates look like yet, because they haven't arrived."

"I'm going to bring Patch," said Laura Baker. She was seven years old and had three rabbits — Nibbles, Fluffy, and Patch.

"And I'll bring Hoppy," added Jack Gardiner. Jack was Laura's best friend. Fluffy was both Patch and Hoppy's mother.

"I'd like to come," said Paul Stevens. "But I haven't got a rabbit." Paul had an Exmoor pony called Paddy.

"You can borrow Fluffy if you like," Laura offered. "And someone else can bring Nibbles."

Everyone started to talk about where they would get a rabbit from. It seemed as if the whole school was going to go to the Bunny Bonanza!

*   *   *

After school, Mandy and James raced to James's house to collect Blackie. Then they set off to deliver posters around the village. They dropped one poster off at the general store and one at the house where Reverend Hadcroft lived. As they came running out of his driveway, they almost bumped into a plump lady who was wearing a large hat and a flowery dress.

"Sorry, Mrs. Ponsonby," gasped Mandy, stopping in her tracks.

The fluffy Pekingese dog under the lady's arm started to yap excitedly.

"Really, children!" Mrs. Ponsonby frowned. "Such dreadful behavior! Look how you've upset my poor Pandora."

Blackie strained on his leash, eager to say hello to the little dog. James struggled to pull him back.

Mrs. Ponsonby looked at Mandy sharply. "I hope you haven't been bothering that nice Reverend Hadcroft."

"We were just delivering a poster," Mandy explained.

"A poster?" Nothing happened in Welford without Mrs. Ponsonby knowing about it. "What for?" she demanded.

Mandy explained about the Bunny Bonanza.

"Oh, I see, a children's event," sniffed Mrs. Ponsonby. "Well, I suppose it's for a good cause."

Blackie was still pulling at his leash. Mrs. Ponsonby turned on James. "James Hunter! Can't you control that dog?"

"I'm trying," said poor James.

"Blackie just wants to say hello," said Mandy, seeing James's embarrassment. "Maybe if you put Pandora down, Mrs. Ponsonby?"

Suddenly Blackie lunged forward. James gasped as the leash slipped through his fingers. Free at last, Blackie jumped joyfully up to sniff Pandora, leaving two large, muddy footprints right on the front of Mrs. Ponsonby's flowery dress.

Mrs. Ponsonby looked down and shrieked loudly.

James and Mandy looked at each other in horror.

"James Hunter!" Mrs. Ponsonby cried angrily. "Look what your dog has done!"

Taking one look at Mrs. Ponsonby's angry, red face, Blackie ran off up the path. Mandy raced after him, leaving James stammering apologies to Mrs. Ponsonby.

Just as Mandy grabbed Blackie's leash, a friendly figure appeared at the front door. "Is everything all right, Mandy? It sounds like World War Three is going on out there."

"Oh, Reverend Hadcroft," gasped Mandy. "It's Mrs. Ponsonby. Blackie just jumped up on her and he left footprints all over her dress!"

Reverend Hadcroft was a young man, with dark curly hair. He started to smile. "Oh, dear. So James needs rescuing, then? Leave it to me."

He strode down the path. Holding tightly on to Blackie's leash, Mandy followed.

"Your dog is a disgrace, James Hunter!" Mrs. Ponsonby was squawking loudly. "An utter disgrace. You should be —"

"Ah, Mrs. Ponsonby," interrupted Reverend Hadcroft. "What a pleasant surprise."

Seeing Reverend Hadcroft, Mrs. Ponsonby stopped in her tracks. "Reverend Hadcroft," she said, adjusting her hat with a sudden smile. "How nice to see you."

"Now, what seems to be the problem?" asked Reverend Hadcroft.

Mrs. Ponsonby started to explain.

"Dear, dear," said Reverend Hadcroft, shaking his head. "What a dreadful shock for you, Mrs. Ponsonby. Why don't you come into the house? You can tell me all about it over a nice cup of tea."

"Really, Reverend, I wouldn't want to trouble you," said Mrs. Ponsonby.

"No trouble at all," said Reverend Hadcroft, winking at Mandy and James as he led Mrs. Ponsonby away.

"Phew!" James said to Mandy. "Thank goodness for Reverend Hadcroft."

"Oh, Blackie," said Mandy looking down at

the dog. "When are you going to learn to behave?"

Blackie wagged his tail. He seemed very pleased with himself.

They hurried him off down the street before Blackie could get into any more trouble. "So what's left on the list of things to do?" asked James as they reached the village square.

"Well, we've done the posters, the labels, and the rabbit food," said Mandy, getting out her list and checking them off.

"I can do the entry forms on my computer tonight," said James. "And start on the signs to go by the runs," he added.

"Then it's just organizing the runs, and finding food and water containers," said Mandy. "Where can we get containers from?"

They looked at each other. They'd both had exactly the same idea!

Grandpa was weeding in the garden. "Come to help?" he asked as they ran in through the gate of Lilac Cottage with Blackie bounding beside them.

"Well, we *hadn't*," said Mandy, kneeling down beside him and passing him the bucket. "But we will. What we really wanted was for you to help us."

Grandpa's eyes twinkled. "What is it this time?" he said. "Not more hamsters or guinea pigs to look after?"

Mandy shook her head and grinned. Grandma and Grandpa had looked after several animals that Mandy had needed to find temporary homes for.

Mandy explained about the food and water containers. "I'm sure I can find you something," said Grandpa. He thought for a moment. "Now, let me see," he said, standing up and walking to the greenhouse.

He reappeared very soon, holding some large saucers. "How about these? They're really for standing flowerpots on," he said. "Would they do?"

"Perfect!" said Mandy.

Grandpa smiled. "There's some newspaper in the house we can use to wrap them in. Then you can take them home," he said. He winked at James. "And we might just find some ginger cookies at the same time!"

Grandma was cleaning the kitchen. She put down her cloth when she saw them. "This is a nice surprise," she said. "Come in and sit down."

"I'll get the cookies," said Grandpa, getting a cookie jar down off the shelf.

Mandy told her grandparents all about the preparations for the Bunny Bonanza. "Everyone at school wants to come," Mandy said happily.

"And they're going to borrow rabbits if they don't own one themselves," said James, taking a cookie from the jar. "We're going to make lots of money for Animal Welfare."

"What about refreshments?" said Grandma.

Mandy and James looked at each other. "Oh, we hadn't thought of that," said James.

"Well, people will need food and drinks,"

said Grandma. "And you can sell them to make more money. Would you like me to bake you some cookies and cakes and set up a little booth?"

"Yes, please!" said Mandy.

"And you'll need some tables and chairs," said Grandpa. "I could get those organized for you. There's some in the village hall. I could ask the Jacksons at Rose Cottage if I could borrow their horse trailer to fetch them in. After all, it's for a good cause."

Mandy hugged him. "You're the best grand-parents in the world!"

Grandpa smiled and ran his hand through his thick white hair. "Now, how many chairs will you need?"

James started to figure it out. "Well, there's Jack and Laura, and Paul Stevens if he brings Fluffy . . ."

"And Jenny and Amy, and Pam said she would come with her cousin's rabbit . . ." Mandy went on.

"And Andrew Pearson and Peter Foster if they borrow rabbits . . ."

"*Lots* of people!" Grandpa laughed. "Right. I'll see what I can do!"

Mandy and James smiled at each other. "I think our Bunny Bonanza is going to be a suc-cess," said James.

"A great success!" Mandy grinned.

7

Parsley

The next morning, Laura Baker came up to Mandy, looking terribly disappointed. "I can't come," she said. "Mom says, since it's Easter, we have to visit my aunt and uncle."

"That's okay," said Mandy.

"But Patch would have loved it!" said Laura.

Paul Stevens overheard them. "I can't come

either," he said. "My mom and dad want to go out for the day."

"So do mine," said Pam Stanton, coming up. "I'm really sorry, Mandy."

"Oh, it's all right," said Mandy. She was trying to sound as if she didn't really mind, but her heart sank. Fewer people meant less money for Animal Welfare.

All day people kept coming up and saying that they couldn't come to the Bunny Bonanza after all. By the end of school, Mandy and James were feeling very glum.

"What are we going to do?" Mandy said as they walked home together. "Oh, James, it doesn't look like it's going to be a Bunny *Bonanza* after all!"

Mandy walked unhappily into Animal Ark reception. Jean and Simon looked up in surprise. Normally Mandy came bounding in.

"Is anything the matter, dear?" Jean asked, sounding concerned.

"Hardly anyone from school's going to be

able to come to our Bunny Bonanza," said Mandy, dumping her schoolbag on the floor. "They're all busy."

"Well, what about other people?" said Jean. "You could put up some more posters."

"But where?" asked Mandy.

"You should put an ad in the local paper," said Simon. "They run them free for small events."

Mandy brightened up. "How do I do that?"

"Call them up," said Simon. "The number's normally on the back page. You might get people from Walton coming then."

"I bet there's an old newspaper in the house!" said Mandy, grabbing her bag. "It's a really good idea. Thanks, Simon!"

Mandy found an old copy of the *Walton Gazette* in the sitting room. She turned quickly to the back. Yes, there it was:

Are you organizing a local event? Let us know and we'll print the details for free. Call Fiona at the Gazette.

*　　*　　*

With shaking hands, Mandy picked up the phone and dialed the number. It rang three times, then she got through.

"Hello, *Walton Gazette*," said a cheerful voice. "This is Fiona speaking. How may I help you?"

"Hello," said Mandy. "My name's Mandy Hope. I'm organizing a local event . . ."

She went on to explain about the Bunny Bonanza. Fiona was very interested and asked quite a lot of questions. "And you're nine years old?" she asked.

"I'm nine and James, who's also organizing it, is eight."

"Okay, Mandy. Well, we'll certainly put details of the Bunny Bonanza into the next edition. We may even mention you in one of our 'Things to do during Easter' features — it sounds like a lovely idea. Now, give me your phone number."

Mandy gave her both the clinic and home numbers. Her heart was turning somersaults by the time she put the phone down. It had been a bit nerve-racking, but Fiona had been really nice. Best of all, it looked like Bunny Bonanza was going to be in the *Walton Gazette*.

Mandy raced back to tell Jean and Simon what she had done. "See, problem solved," said Simon. "You're sure to get more people now."

"Particularly if the newspaper mentions you in a feature," added Jean.

Mandy crossed her fingers. "Oh, I really hope they do!"

The next edition of the newspaper was not due out until Friday, and Mandy and James could hardly wait. As soon as school was finished on Friday, they raced to Animal Ark. "It's here!" said Jean, holding up the week's edition of the *Walton Gazette*.

"Are we in it?" gasped Mandy.

Jean handed them the paper, which was open at a page near the back. There was a big headline: LOCAL EVENTS.

Mandy and James looked down the column labeled EASTER SATURDAY.

"There we are!" squealed Mandy.

Sure enough, there was a little box with all the details about the Bunny Bonanza. The newspaper had even added a little drawing of a rabbit.

"And look!" said James, pointing excitedly at the article in the middle of the page. "*Look!*"

The article was called WHAT TO DO ON EASTER WEEKEND. Halfway down, it said:

For a fun day out on Easter Saturday, why not go to Welford village square, where the Welford Bunny Bonanza is being held. Organizers Mandy Hope (9) and James Hunter (8) are planning to gather as many rabbits as possible together for a photograph in aid of Animal Welfare. Take your rabbits along and get your certificate!

Mandy gasped as she read it. "It's great — we'll get loads of people now!"

"Remember that not everyone reads the back pages," said Jean. "But you should at least get a few more."

Mandy and James decided to visit Jenny to tell her the good news, because she was really interested in the Bunny Bonanza. "We can see Clover and her babies," said Mandy. "And check that Jenny is going to bring them all to the Bunny Bonanza."

"I wonder if she's chosen which one to keep yet," said James as they walked there. "If I were her, I wouldn't know *how* to choose."

Jenny was sitting in a large open-topped run, playing with the baby rabbits. Mandy and James quickly told her about the *Walton Gazette*. "It will be so good if there are lots of rabbits there," she said, delighted.

James looked at the baby rabbits. "Have you decided which one to keep yet?"

"That one," said Jenny, pointing to a small

white one with dark-gray ears. "I'm going to call him Parsley."

"He's so cute," said Mandy, looking at the baby rabbit hopping around the run. "Can I hold him?"

"Of course," said Jenny. "Come in."

James and Mandy both stepped carefully into the run. The little rabbits scattered everywhere, their noses twitched, and their tiny ears pricked up. Mandy and James both knew how to pick up a rabbit — using the scruff of the neck and then quickly supporting the rabbit's bottom with the other hand. Mandy picked up Parsley. The little rabbit nestled against her and she gently stroked the top of his head.

"He's lovely," said Mandy softly.

"Is Amy taking one?" James asked Jenny.

Jenny grinned. "Yes, she finally persuaded her mom. She's taking that one," she said, pointing to a black one with silver tips that looked just like a tiny Clover. "She's going to call her Tulip."

James picked up Tulip. "I wonder what

Minnie will think of her?" he said, thinking about Amy's white mouse. "I hope they'll be friends."

"Are you still going to bring them all to the Bunny Bonanza?" asked Mandy.

"I don't think I can," said Jenny. "Mom thinks it will be too many for me to look after. She's said I can bring Clover and Parsley, and Amy's going to bring Tulip, but that's all."

"Never mind," said James, seeing Mandy's disappointment. "Lots of other rabbits will come when their owners see the ad."

"But Jean doesn't think lots of people *will* read it," said Mandy doubtfully.

Just then, Mrs. Carter came out of the house. "Hello," she said, smiling at Mandy and James. "I thought I heard you two out here. I've just been putting together some packs for the rabbits' new owners."

"Packs?" said James.

"Yes, they contain information. Come and see."

James, Mandy, and Jenny followed Mrs. Carter into the house. She handed each of them a plastic envelope. They looked inside. There was a diet sheet explaining what to feed the rabbits, plus a pedigree certificate and a leaflet about vaccinating rabbits.

"This is really good," said James. He was impressed. "The new owners will know everything they need to know."

"That's what I hope," said Mrs. Carter. "I try to give them as much information as possible."

Mandy had a sudden idea. "Dad has some leaflets in the clinic about how to look after pet rabbits," she said. "Would you like me to get you some? You could put one in each pack."

Mrs. Carter smiled. "That's a really good idea. Thank you, Mandy."

"I'll go and get them," said Mandy. "It won't take long."

Leaving James with Jenny and the babies, Mandy set off for Animal Ark.

*　　*　　*

"I've just come to get some rabbit leaflets for Mrs. Carter," she explained to Jean, who was sitting at reception.

"Okay," said Jean. Just then, the phone rang.

"Animal Ark," said Jean, picking up the receiver. There was a moment's silence while the other person spoke. "Mandy Hope?" said Jean, surprised. "Are you sure you don't mean *Emily* Hope? Emily Hope is the vet. Mandy is her daughter." Mandy looked around. There was another pause. "Oh, I see," said Jean. "Yes. Well, it *is* Mandy you want, then. If you wait a moment I'll put her on."

Jean covered the mouthpiece of the phone and beckoned Mandy over. She looked excited. "It's someone from a newspaper!" she said, her glasses slipping down her nose.

"The *Walton Gazette*?" asked Mandy, puzzled.

"No! The *Yorkshire Chronicle*," said Jean. "It's a much bigger paper, sold all over Yorkshire. Guess what? They want to speak to you about the Bunny Bonanza!"

8

An Interview

Mandy put down the phone. Her eyes were shining with excitement. "The *Yorkshire Chronicle* wants to do an article on the Bunny Bonanza!" she gasped. "They want to interview James and me here tomorrow. And they want us to find some rabbits for a photograph!"

Jean's glasses fell right off her nose. "They're coming *here* to take photographs tomorrow?"

"Yes!" said Mandy. "After morning office hours. I have to go and tell James!" She grabbed the leaflets and raced back to the Carters' house at top speed.

James and Jenny could hardly believe the news. "Could we use Clover and her babies for the photograph, please?" Mandy asked Jenny.

"I'll ask Mom," said Jenny excitedly. "It would be great!"

Mrs. Carter said they could use the babies. She even offered to bring them around to Animal Ark for Mandy and James. "What time do you want them?" she asked.

"One o'clock," said Mandy.

"Okay. We'll be there twenty minutes before."

Waving good-bye to Jenny and Mrs. Carter, Mandy and James set off for home. "See you tomorrow!" Mandy called to James as they went in their separate directions.

"One o'clock sharp," said James. He grinned. "I can't wait!"

The next morning Jean came into Animal Ark wearing a very pretty new skirt and bright pink lipstick. Simon's hair was brushed firmly in place. During morning office hours, Jean tidied the reception area from top to bottom — even dusting the flea sprays and worming tablets.

"Aren't you going to brush your hair, dear?" she asked Mandy, who was helping Simon sweep and mop the floor after the last patient left.

Mandy quickly ran a hand through her short blond hair and laughed. She hardly ever bothered with her clothes or hair. "They'll be looking at the rabbits, not me!" she said.

"Only a quarter of an hour and then they'll be here," said Simon.

Mandy frowned. "I hope Mrs. Carter arrives soon."

The door burst open and James came running in. "Is the paper here yet?" he gasped.

Mandy shook her head and squeezed out her mop. "No and neither is Mrs. Carter. She's late." Jean started dusting the posters on the wall.

Dr. Adam came through from the residential unit. He looked around the spotless reception area and his eyes twinkled. "Maybe we should get a newspaper reporter here every day," he said. "I've never seen this place look so nice!"

"Dad," said Mandy anxiously, "Mrs. Carter hasn't arrived yet and the people from the paper will be here soon!"

Simon looked out of the clinic window. "They're here!"

"Quick!" said Jean, shuffling the papers on the desk. "Is everything tidy?"

The clinic door opened. In walked a woman with a clipboard and a man with a camera. The woman had short dark hair and big red glasses. "Hi, I'm Sue from the *Yorkshire Chronicle*," she said brightly. She smiled broadly at Mandy. "You must be Mandy Hope."

Mandy blushed and nodded. "Yes, and this is my friend, James Hunter."

Sue held out her hand. "Pleased to meet you, James." James shook hands and mumbled a rather embarrassed hello. Sue looked around at the adults. "And who else have we got here?"

Jean and Simon grinned from the reception desk.

"Hi!" said Simon. Jean just giggled.

"This is Jean, the Animal Ark receptionist," Mandy explained quickly. "And Simon . . ."

"The practice nurse," said Simon, smoothing down his hair.

Dr. Adam came forward. "I'm Adam Hope, Mandy's father."

"Super!" said Sue shaking his hand. She looked around. "Now, where are these rabbits?"

Mandy gulped nervously. "Umm . . ."

Just then the door flew open and a rather breathless Mrs. Carter and Jenny arrived. "Sorry! We had trouble starting the car," Mrs. Carter said. She was carrying a large cardboard box. "Here are the babies."

Within a few minutes, Sue had them all organized. Mandy and James were posed standing against a wall near their poster. James had to hold the box of rabbits and Mandy had to cuddle Parsley and Clover, with Jean sitting behind the desk and Simon leaning on the counter. Jenny and Mrs. Carter grinned at them all from behind Sue.

"Now, Dr. Adam," said Sue. "If we can have you right here."

Dr. Adam cleared his throat. "Well . . ."

"Now, no being shy," insisted Sue. "I need you right here behind Jean. Come on, right here!" Mandy grinned as she saw her dad move meekly to where Sue wanted him. She didn't seem prepared to take no for an answer. "Yes, there," she cried. "That's it, a little bit closer — *super*!"

"Just look at the camera," she said. "One, two, three, and *smile*!"

The man with her took lots of photographs. "My arms are dropping off!" James muttered to Mandy.

"Parsley keeps trying to crawl up my arm," whispered Mandy.

"Smile!" called Sue for about the tenth time. Mandy and James stretched their mouths into wide grins.

"Here we go. . . ."

At last the photos were done. The interview was much easier. Sue sat down with Mandy

and James and asked them how they'd gotten the idea for the Bunny Bonanza, what charity it was for, and when and where it was to be held. To James's relief, Mandy did most of the talking.

"Great!" said Sue, standing up when the interview was over. "I think I've got all I need. We'll be along to photograph the event. People can order photos afterward if they want to." Mandy and James followed her outside to wave good-bye. "The story will be in the paper on Wednesday, so look out for it!" she said, getting into her car.

Mandy turned to James. "The day school ends for the holidays!"

"And only three days before the Bunny Bonanza," he reminded her as Sue drove off.

"Mandy Hope, James Hunter!" They looked around to see Mrs. Ponsonby striding purposefully toward them. Pandora was tucked firmly under her arm as usual.

"That car had *Yorkshire Chronicle* written on the side," she announced as she reached them.

"Was it someone from the newspaper? What did they want?"

"It was a reporter, Mrs. Ponsonby," Mandy explained. "She came to interview us for the newspaper because she'd heard about the Bunny Bonanza."

"That rabbit event you've been organizing?" questioned Mrs. Ponsonby.

Mandy nodded.

"Yes, the *Yorkshire Chronicle* is going to come and take photos of it," James said.

"Photographs? For the newspaper?" Mrs. Ponsonby straightened up and looked down at Pandora. "I didn't know there would be newspaper photographs. In that case, darling Pandora will certainly attend."

Mandy gulped. "But, Mrs. Ponsonby, the Bunny Bonanza's not for dogs. Pandora might upset the rabbits."

Mrs. Ponsonby glared at Mandy. "My little Pandora, upset the rabbits? Nonsense!"

"But —" began Mandy.

It was too late. Mrs. Ponsonby had sailed on down the street, her nose in the air.

Mandy and James looked at each other. "That's all we need," said James. "Mrs. Ponsonby bringing Pandora."

"At least we know now that *one* person will be coming," said Mandy, looking on the bright side.

"But Mrs. Ponsonby!" said James. "Help!"

On Wednesday afternoon, Mandy and James raced back to Animal Ark after school. The *Yorkshire Chronicle* was lying on the front mat. They grabbed it and flipped through the pages. "Here!" cried Mandy. "Look, James."

There was a big black-and-white photograph of them. Above it was the headline BUNNY BONANZA! and below it was an article containing all the details.

"Look what it says about us!" said James. He read out loud, "'Full credit should go to youngsters Mandy Hope and James Hunter for their imaginative idea to raise money for Animal Welfare.'" He broke off to grin at Mandy.

She read on quickly. "'The Bunny Bonanza promises to be one of the most interesting and certainly most worthwhile events over the Easter weekend. Take your rabbits along for a day of fun — go to the Welford Bunny Bonanza!'" Her blue eyes shone. "This is bound to make people come!"

The phone rang. It was Laura Baker. "Mandy, it's me!" she said in excitement. "My mom's just seen the paper and she said I can come to the Bunny Bonanza after all — my aunt and uncle are going to come, too!"

"That's great!" said Mandy.

"Patch will be so pleased," said Laura.

No sooner had Mandy put down the phone than it rang again. It was Paul Stevens. "Mom's seen the article on the Bunny Bonanza and thinks we should stay here to support it. She said she never realized it was going to be such a big thing. I'm going to be able to come!"

"Terrific!" said Mandy.

Five minutes later the phone rang again. This time it was Jenny. "Everyone's been calling me up to see if they can borrow Clover's babies to take to the Bunny Bonanza. Oh, Mandy, the babies are all going to be able to come after all!"

Mandy and James told Simon and Jean the good news. Then they raced around to Lilac Cottage to tell Grandma and Grandpa.

"It sounds like it should be really quite busy," said Grandma.

"You're going to need some helpers," said Grandpa. "People to collect money and show people where to go and what to do."

"But all our friends are bringing rabbits," Mandy said anxiously. "They won't be able to help. What should we do?"

Grandma winked at her. "I think if you asked Grandpa nicely he might be able to think of something."

"Oh, Grandpa," said Mandy, going around

the table and putting her arms around him, "would you help?"

"Of course, love," said Grandpa. "And I might even be able to persuade a few of my friends to come along and help as well. I'll ask Walter Pickard and Mike Jordan."

"I've asked my friend Kathy to help, too," said Grandma.

"Oh, good!" said Mandy. She liked Kathy. Kathy kept chickens and had given Mandy some advice when she and James had hatched a duckling from an egg. They had called it Dilly.

"So, it looks like we're all organized," said Grandma.

The next few days sped by for Mandy and James. They visited all their friends with rabbits and guinea pigs who lived near Lilac Cottage, and asked if they could borrow their wire-mesh runs. They then had to spend most of Friday afternoon bringing the runs over to Lilac Cottage to be put into the horse trailer along with the chairs and tables. The certificates arrived and were packed into a box with the entry forms, pens, money containers, and labels.

"I'll bring the signs on my bike," said James.

"We'll meet at twelve o'clock," said Mandy. "That gives us two whole hours to set up."

Mandy ate supper that night with her mom. Her dad was out on a call. "It's all going to go so well," Mandy said, cutting a slice of quiche.

"We're going to make loads of money for animals and everyone will have lots of fun!"

Dr. Emily frowned thoughtfully. "You know, I hope there aren't too many people and rabbits," she said.

"How could there be too many?" said Mandy, amazed. "The more there are, the more money we make for Animal Welfare, and the more fun it will be!"

"It could get rather chaotic," warned Dr. Emily.

"We've organized things really well," Mandy said confidently. "And anyway, you and Dad and Simon and Jean are all going to be there, *and* Grandma and Grandpa. Loads of us!"

Dr. Adam came through the door just as Mandy was speaking. He'd been out on a visit to Woodbridge Farm Park, performing an emergency operation on a goat, who had swallowed a piece of rusty wire. "I'm really sorry, but I won't be there tomorrow, love," he said to Mandy. "I'm going to have to go back to the farm after office hours to check on the goat."

"Is he all right?" Mandy asked anxiously.

"He'll make it," said Adam Hope. "There was no real damage to his insides, but I do need to see him tomorrow. I'm sorry about not being able to make it for your Bunny Bonanza, though."

Mandy was very disappointed, but she understood that her dad had to see the goat. Sick animals always came first. "Never mind," she said, getting up and giving him a hug. "Everyone else can still help, and with so much help what can go wrong?"

9

The Big Day!

Grandpa drove up to Animal Ark in the Jacksons' Land Rover. The horse trailer was hitched to the back. "Everything ready?" Grandpa asked as Mandy came hurrying out of the house.

"Yes, I've got the entry forms, labels, pens,

money containers, and certificates in here," Mandy said. She had checked and rechecked the box and even put in a camera, just in case the *Yorkshire Chronicle* didn't turn up. It would be awful not to have any photos of the big day!

Grandpa got out and opened the side door of the trailer. It was filled with folding chairs, tables, and wire-mesh runs. Mandy carefully placed the box inside and then scrambled into the back of the Land Rover. "Hi, Grandma! Isn't it lovely and sunny?"

"Perfect," agreed Grandma. "Careful you don't lean on any of those cakes."

Next to Mandy, the seat was piled high with cake and cookie boxes, and cardboard boxes filled with plates and glasses.

Grandpa got in. "Right!" he said, looking around at them and rubbing his hands together. "Let's go!"

When they got to the village square, they saw James waiting there with Blackie.

"Mom wanted him out of the house while she did some cleaning up," James explained as Mandy ran over to him. "I'll take him home before people start arriving. There's bound to be enough time."

They tied up Blackie to a tree by the Land Rover. James gave him his new toy. It was stuffed with treats. "He hasn't chewed a thing since we got this," said James. "Mom thinks it's great."

Grandpa took down the back of the trailer and started to unload the tables and chairs. Mandy and James ran around to help. The tables were very heavy. "Where should we put them?" James puffed to Mandy.

"We need one for the food and one for entries," said Mandy. "The rest can be for people to sit at."

They set out the refreshment table first. Grandma started unpacking the plates and glasses. Her friend Kathy came hurrying across the square with a large basket full of cakes.

"Isn't it a lovely day?" she said, looking up at the blue sky. "So sunny."

"How's Lala?" Mandy asked. Lala was Kathy's beautiful, but deaf, Siamese cat. Kathy had given her a home when Lala's previous owners had moved abroad.

"Very well, thank you, Mandy." Kathy smiled.

James nudged Mandy. "Look! Is that some people arriving already?"

A car had drawn up by the green. People were getting out with a rabbit carrier.

"We'd better get a move on," Mandy said, alarmed. They hurried back to the trailer. Luckily, Walter Pickard and Mike Jordan had arrived. They were helping Grandpa carry the tables. "We'll do the rabbit area!" called Mandy.

Mandy and James dragged the rabbit runs over to the shade beneath the old oak tree. Mandy knelt down and started crawling slowly over the grass. "What *are* you doing?" James asked in amazement.

"Checking for buttercups — they're poisonous for rabbits," explained Mandy. "But I think it looks okay."

They set out the runs and the water containers. James borrowed a hammer from Grandpa. "I'll put up the signs," he said. He had made three. There was one that said RABBIT FOOD, and one that said PLEASE KEEP YOUR RABBITS IN THE SHADE. Another had a list of rules for using the runs.

While James put up the signs, Mandy ran across to the general store to pick up the old vegetables Mrs. McFarlane had promised to collect from her friend's shop.

Mrs. McFarlane brought out a sack of cabbage and carrots from the back room. "It looks like you're going to be quite busy today!" she said to Mandy. "I've had lots of questions." She smiled. "It's for such a good cause."

Mandy hurried back to tell James. By the time she got back to the square, more people had arrived. They were unloading their rabbits and lining up for refreshments.

"There must be at least fifteen people here already," said James. "And it doesn't start for . . ." He looked at his watch. ". . . for another hour."

"We should set up the entry table," said Mandy. "Then people can start filling in their forms."

James frowned. "It doesn't look like I'll have time to take Blackie home after all."

"He'll be fine," said Mandy, looking over to where Blackie was lying in the shade chewing the treats out of his toy. "He looks quite happy."

Mandy and James started to put the entry forms and certificates out on a table.

A couple of people walked over. "Are you taking entries now?" they asked.

Mandy nodded eagerly. "It's one dollar for each rabbit," she said. "Will you fill in one of these forms, please?" She handed each person a form. They filled them in and handed them back with two dollars.

James handed them each a label. "The photograph will be at three o'clock," he said.

Mandy turned to James as the people walked
off. "Our first entries!" she said in delight.

"And here come lots more!" said James,
pointing to a crowd of people who were heading straight for them.

A line quickly formed. Mandy felt a smile
fixing on her face as she greeted one new per-

son after another and handed out form after form. The people just seemed to keep coming.

"It's one dollar per rabbit," she said automatically, reaching for a form as the next person in the line moved up to the desk.

"Mandy, it's us!" Jenny and Amy laughed.

"Oops!" said Mandy. "Sorry. It's just that there've been so many people."

"We can tell," said Amy. "There are loads! Look at them all."

Mandy looked around. There were people hanging around the refreshment booth, putting rabbits in the runs, sitting on rugs on the grass, lining up to fill in their entries.

"Mandy!" said James, nudging her and nodding at the line of people who were starting to look restless at the delay.

"I'd better not talk now," Mandy said quickly. "Here are the forms."

Amy and Jenny filled them in. Amy had Tulip, and Jenny had Clover and Parsley. They handed in their money and James gave them each a sticker. "See you later!" they called. Mandy handed the next person a form.

"Mandy, I don't think we're going to have enough certificates," James said. He was looking rather worried.

Mandy stared at him. "We have to!"

"We've only got fifty," said James. "And almost all the entry forms have been used. That means there must be almost fifty people entered already."

The people next in the line spoke rather loudly to Mandy. "Do you think we could have some entry forms, please!"

"Oh . . . yes . . . sorry," said Mandy, quickly handing them two entry forms. She noticed as she did so that James was right: The pile *was* almost gone, and there were lots of people still in the line.

Amy and Jenny came running back to the table. Their faces were worried. "Mandy!" they gasped. "Some people keep trying to put all different rabbits in the runs together — girls and boys, and rabbits that don't even know each other!"

Mandy stared at Jenny and Amy in horror. This was serious. It could cause a rabbit fight. "You've got to stop them," she said.

"We tried, but they wouldn't listen!" said Jenny.

Mandy got to her feet.

"Where are you going?" James exclaimed.

"The rabbits need help!" said Mandy.

"You can't leave me with all these people!" James cried.

Mandy looked around in desperation.

"Hello, love."

Mandy swung around and saw her mom and Simon approaching. She had never felt so relieved. "Oh, Mom!" she cried. "You've got to help!" She filled her mother in quickly on the story of the rabbits. "There are so many people here! And so many people still to fill in their entry forms!"

"Don't worry," said Dr. Emily calmly. "Simon and I will deal with the rabbits. You carry on here."

"But, Mom, that's not all . . ." said Mandy, but Simon and Dr. Emily had already hurried off in the direction of the rabbit runs.

"I'm *still* waiting for an entry form!" said the next person in the line. Mandy grabbed a form and shoved it into his hand. "It's one dollar for each rabbit!" she gabbled. "Will you fill in this form, please."

"I will, now that you've given it to me," said the man sharply. A couple of people behind him started muttering about how long they had been waiting.

"The certificates!" whispered James anxiously. "Mandy, what are we going to do?"

Grandma came hurrying over. "Mandy, love, we're running out of refreshments. I never dreamed there would be this many people here."

Mandy stared at Grandma and James desperately. Everything was going horribly wrong.

There were just too many people. Mom and Simon were too busy with the rabbits to help, and James and Grandma were looking at her for ideas. If only . . .

Mandy stared at the tall, bearded figure striding toward the table. "*Dad!*" she shrieked. "Oh, I'm so glad you're here."

10

Blackie Saves the Day

"The goat was much better than I thought," Dr. Adam explained. "So I thought I would come down here after all." He looked around the village square. "It all looks very busy."

"It is!" said Mandy. She poured out her troubles. "We need more certificates and we're running out of refreshments. And all these people still need to fill in their entries."

Dr. Adam smiled. "Don't worry. With a bit of teamwork, I'm sure we can soon get things straightened out. Now, how about getting Grandma to call up her Women's Club friends on my cell phone, to see if they can help with extra refreshments?"

"Brilliant!" said Mandy.

Grandma's friends were only too happy to help. They promised to bring cookies, cakes, and drinks down to the village square as soon as possible.

"What are the other problems?" said Dr. Adam.

"The line," said Mandy.

"And we're running out of entry forms, and we won't have enough certificates," put in James.

"You could photocopy some more," suggested Dr. Adam.

"But it's too far to get to Animal Ark and back," Mandy objected. Her eyes suddenly lit up. "But Mrs. McFarlane has a copy machine in the general store. I wonder if she would let me use it?"

"Why don't you go and see?" said Dr. Adam. "I'll get Grandpa and Walter Pickard to set up another entry table. That will make the line shorter."

Mandy raced to the general store. Mrs. McFarlane was very helpful. "I've had lots of people from your Bunny Bonanza in here buying candy and newspapers," she said. "It's been very good for business. Make as many copies as you need."

Five minutes later, Mandy emerged on the village square with a whole batch of freshly copied certificates and entry forms. She put a handful on each entry table and set about helping James again. With two tables, the lines quickly went down.

Amy and Jenny came over just as Mandy and James dealt with the last person waiting. "Just look, Mandy," Jenny said. "Absolutely *everyone's* here!"

Mandy looked around. As well as all the strangers, for the first time she saw all her school friends. "They've all got rabbits!" Mandy exclaimed. She had never seen so many rabbits all together — there were rabbits being supervised in the runs by her mom and Simon, rabbits in their carriers, rabbits being cuddled, and rabbits nibbling on the vegetables that Mrs. McFarlane had provided.

Dr. Adam left his table and came over. "Sue from the newspaper has just arrived. I think you two should go and say hello."

James and Mandy went over to where Sue and the photographer were setting up a camera and tripod. "Super!" Sue said when she saw them. "Just the two people I wanted to see. Now, are you ready to get this photograph under way? It's almost three o'clock. I've got a microphone here — it will help you to be heard. You just turn it on like this," she said, handing it to Mandy and showing her a switch. "Could you get everyone over here in a semi-circle?"

Mandy held the microphone and looked at her dad and James. "Go on," James urged her.

Mandy cleared her throat and switched on the microphone. "Hello, everyone." Her voice boomed out of the speaker, loud and crackly. James grinned at her. "Welcome to the Bunny Bonanza," Mandy continued. "We are about to take the group photograph. Could you all bring your rabbits over here, please?"

There was a bustle of movement as people started to take their rabbits out of their carriers and come toward her.

Mandy's eyes suddenly widened. "James, look!"

Heading across the square toward them was Mrs. Ponsonby. In her arms was Pandora, and on Pandora's head was a pair of furry rabbit ears. "Where's this photograph going to be?" she demanded loudly. "I want a good position for my little Pandora."

"But, Mrs. Ponsonby," Mandy began. "It's a Bunny Bonanza. It's not for dogs . . ."

Just then, Mandy heard Grandpa shout out.

She looked around. Blackie had pulled his leash free from the tree. Like a streak of black lightning he came racing around the Land Rover and across the grass toward them. He had seen Pandora and Mrs. Ponsonby.

"Blackie! Come!" shouted James, but Blackie ignored him.

The little Pekingese leaped wildly in Mrs. Ponsonby's arms. "Pandora, darling! *No!*" Mrs. Ponsonby shrieked as Pandora wriggled free and fell to the ground. Pandora was off, running across the ground, with Blackie chasing after her in hot pursuit.

The two dogs raced straight through the crowd of people. The air was filled with screams as people dropped their rabbits and the rabbits scattered in all directions.

"Oh, no!" Mandy gasped in horror. "What are we going to do?"

People started to run after the escaping rabbits. Mandy knew that running was the worst thing the owners could do — the rabbits

would just panic! She looked around in desperation and suddenly saw the microphone. Grabbing it, she pushed the switch. "Stop!" she cried, her voice crackling out. "Don't run!"

People stopped.

"Just stay still," Mandy urged. "Try and get the rabbits to come to you. If you run, they'll run faster!"

People crouched down and started tempting the rabbits toward them. One by one, the rabbits were caught and reunited with their relieved owners. Dr. Adam caught Pandora and handed her back to Mrs. Ponsonby. James was at the far side of the square trying to catch an excited Blackie.

"Quick thinking," Sue said, coming up to Mandy and patting her on the back. "Well done, Mandy."

Mandy looked with relief at the rabbits, now safe in their owners' arms. But just then Jenny Carter came running up. "Clover!" she said. "I've lost Clover."

Mandy's heart sank. She scanned the square.

"There!" she gasped, pointing to where the small black rabbit was hopping across the square and toward the road.

Jenny and Mandy started to run around the crowd. But it was too late. They would never reach Clover in time.

"James!" Mandy shouted desperately as the rabbit hopped past James and Blackie. "Stop Clover!"

Everyone fell silent. James and Blackie looked around. Blackie woofed, and before James could grab him he was flying across the grass. He ran straight in front of the rabbit and stopped, dropping his head on his paws and sticking his bottom in the air.

Clover stopped dead.

Blackie wagged his tail.

"Blackie, stay!" gasped James. Blackie flopped into a lying-down position. His eyes never left Clover. James reached them and put his hands on Blackie's collar. The little rabbit stared in fear.

Mandy and Jenny crept up behind. "Clover!"

Jenny called softly. The little rabbit looked around. She hesitated for a moment and then turned and hopped straight into Jenny's open arms.

Everyone in the village square cheered. James and Blackie were quickly surrounded. Blackie was hugged and stroked and patted. "He's a hero," cried Mandy. "He stopped Clover from going onto the road."

"What a clever dog!" said Grandma.

"Thank you, Blackie. Thank you *so* much!" said Jenny, hugging Clover close.

"What a story!" said Sue.

Once everyone was quite sure there were no more missing rabbits, Sue set about organizing everyone into a semicircle with their rabbits. "Two rows please. Little ones at the front, tall ones at the back. Now, hold on *tightly* to your rabbits." Everyone got into position. Sue placed two chairs in the center of the semicircle.

"Take your seats," she said to James and Mandy. "And let's have Blackie in the middle."

As James, Mandy, and Blackie walked to their chairs, everyone cheered. Even Mrs. Ponsonby clapped her hands and smiled. "What a clever young dog," she said to Mandy's grandma in a very loud voice.

James went pink. Mandy grinned happily. Dr. Adam and Dr. Emily, Grandma and Grandpa, and all their friends who had helped came to stand at the end of the two circles. They joined in with the clapping.

"Right!" called Sue. "Now, let's have all the rabbits and owners, and Pandora and Blackie, looking toward the camera. Are we all ready? Now, look at the camera and on the count of three I want you to say 'carrots' — got that? Are you ready? One . . . two . . . three . . ."

"*CARROTS!*" everyone shouted.

It was ages before everyone went home. It was such a nice day that people just seemed to want to stay and chat and eat the delicious cakes and cookies made by Grandma's Women's Club friends. Mandy and James sat on the grass with their friends, eating cookies, playing with the rabbits, and telling Blackie over and over again how clever he was.

At long last, people slowly started leaving. It was time to clean up. James and Mandy hauled themselves off the ground and started to help put all the tables and chairs away in the trailer.

"I'm exhausted!" said James, yawning.

"Just think of all the money we've raised!" said Mandy.

James grinned. "It must be at least a hundred dollars."

"More," said Mandy. "There's the photographs as well."

"And the money from the refreshments," added Grandma, coming past them with a box full of empty cake and cookie boxes.

Mandy and James looked at their friends and their rabbits as they all slowly but happily left the village square. Blackie stood beside them wagging his tail. Dr. Emily came up and put her arms around them both. "So, was it all worth it?" she asked.

Mandy and James looked at each other, grinning. "Oh, yes!" they said.

Mandy's eyes shone. "It really has been the *best* Bunny Bonanza ever!" she said.

Make a New Friend!

Whenever a pet is in trouble, Mandy Hope and her friend James are ready to help.

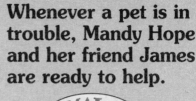